It Is Illegal To Quack Like a Duck

& OTHER FREAKY LAWS

It Is Illegal To Quack Like a Duck
& OTHER FREAKY LAWS

BARBARA SEULING

illustrated by Gwenn Seuling

LODESTAR BOOKS   E. P. DUTTON   NEW YORK

Library of Congress Cataloging-in-Publication Data

Seuling, Barbara.
  It is illegal to quack like a duck and other
freaky laws.

  Includes index.
  Summary: An overview of some unusual laws from all
over the world.
  1. Law—Juvenile literature.   2. Law—United States—
Juvenile literature.   [1. Law]   I. Seuling, Gwenn,
ill.   II.Title.
K183.S48   1988   340   87-31128
ISBN 0-525-67257-5

Published in the United States by E. P. Dutton,
2 Park Avenue, New York, N.Y. 10016,
a division of NAL Penguin Inc.

Published simultaneously in Canada by
Fitzhenry & Whiteside Limited, Toronto

Editor: Virginia Buckley

Printed in the U.S.A.   W   First Edition
10 9 8 7 6 5 4 3 2 1

to my mom,
Helen Veronica Seuling,
and in memory of my dad,
Kaspar Joseph Seuling

Contents

Introduction

Some years ago, after my first book of funny laws, *You Can't Eat Peanuts in Church & Other Little-Known Laws,* was published, I received a lot of mail from people all over the country who thought the book was amusing, but wanted to know: Were those laws for real?

Yes, they were. That, to me, is what made them so funny. And it still does. Sadly, this particular kind of legal history may soon be lost in the dust of time as modern computers weed out outdated, poorly written, and unnecessary laws to make way for new ones. Let me assure you, however, that although the laws that appear in this book may no longer be on the books by the time you read this, they are—or were—for real. I hope that I have salvaged enough of them to give you a few more laughs.

Barbara Seuling
Landgrove, Vermont

1

It's a Dog's Life

☐ In Tuscumbia, Alabama, it is illegal for more than eight rabbits to live on the same block.

☐ In Pacific Grove, California, it is unlawful to threaten a butterfly.

☐ The Maine legislature passed a bill that, in one section, permitted animal humane societies to "destroy old, maimed and disabled horses and other animals." In another section, it stated that the word "animal," as used in the bill, "shall be held to include every living creature."

☐ In South Bend, Indiana, a monkey was tried and convicted for smoking a cigarette.

☐ You may not feed garbage to animals in Boston, Massachusetts.

☐ In Virginia, it is unlawful to alter the mark of an unmarked hog.

☐ An ordinance of 1637 made it unlawful for the colonists of New Amsterdam, later New York, to throw dead animals into the streets.

☐ You cannot ride an ugly horse down the street in Wilbur, Washington, without breaking the law.

☐ No dogs are allowed in Reykjavík, Iceland, except for Seeing Eye dogs.

☐ It is illegal to own any animal as a pet in China. Only animals that are raised for food or for work are lawful.

☐ A dog owner in New Zealand is required by law to take his pet for a walk at least once every twenty-four hours.

☐ Ancient Celtic (Welsh) law states that "whoever shall find a swarm of wild bees is to have a penny or the wax; and the owner of the land is to have the swarm."

☐ A Massachusetts law of 1648 offered any Englishman a reward of thirty shillings for the head of a wolf.

☐ It is against the law in England for an old-clothes dealer to sell an animal to a child.

☐ The law codes of ancient Wales declared: "Whosoever shall sell a cat shall answer for her not going a-caterwauling every moon."

☐ You may not pass through the town of Kiluken, Liberia, carrying a white rooster.

☐ It is unlawful in England to wrestle with an untrained bull in public.

☐ Imitating animals is forbidden in Miami, Florida.

☐ In Phoenix, Arizona, it is illegal to place glass bottles under a horse's feet.

2

Isn't It Romantic?

☐ In Los Angeles, California, you cannot dance with a member of the opposite sex unless you are married.

☐ In Oregon, a girl cannot enter an automobile with a man unless she is chaperoned.

☐ People in Iowa were once required to have liquor cards that had to be punched with each purchase of alcoholic beverages. Parents of young women would check out the character of the young men courting their daughters by asking to see their liquor cards.

☐ In Venice, Italy, it is against the law for gondoliers to play anything besides traditional Venetian songs as they float romantic couples along the city's many canals.

☐ In London, England, it is unlawful to kiss in a movie theater.

☐ You cannot embrace in the street in London, England.

☐ In London, England, lovemaking is not permitted in railway trains, buses, parked motorcars, churchyards, chapels, or parks.

☐ In 1288, Queen Margaret of Scotland decreed that in a leap year any woman could propose to any available man she liked. If he refused her, he would be fined £100.

3

Indiscretions and Embarrassments

☐ You are breaking the law if you leave a mannequin naked in a store window in New York City.

☐ In Chicago, Illinois, it is illegal to hug your neighbor against her wishes.

☐ It is illegal to quack like a duck in the city of Stark, Kansas.

☐ In Greenwich, England, in the 1800s, it was against the law to impersonate a retired person on a pension.

☐ In Delaware, it is unlawful to pretend to be a witch.

☐ In Wichita, Kansas, a city ordinance makes it unlawful to throw talcum powder at anyone.

☐ In Oklahoma, you cannot print a lie in the newspaper to increase sales.

☐ It is illegal in Kentucky to throw eggs at a public speaker.

☐ It was considered a serious offense among the Ba-ila, a Bantu people of central Africa, for a hunter outside the tribe, after killing an elephant, to walk around the back of the animal or to laugh at its buttocks.

☐ It was against the law to insult a rice plant in ancient Cambodia.

☐ It is forbidden in Britain for one member of Parliament to insult another member.

☐ In 1425, a Scottish law was passed prohibiting the importation of the Irish.

☐ In Miriam, South Dakota, it is unlawful to smoke candy cigarettes in any school.

☐ In ancient China, an officer of the court was required to keep a clove in his mouth when talking to his sovereign.

4

The Shirt off
My Back

☐ A person in Cambridge, England, is not allowed to bathe in a river or pond unless he is "wearing suitable drawers."

☐ In Worcester, Massachusetts, it is mandatory for the sheriff to wear a cutaway coat, top hat, and a sword at all murder trials.

☐ It was a crime in fourteenth-century England for a man who earned less than £20 a year to wear a nightcap made of silk.

☐ Sleeping in your day clothing is against the law in Boston, Massachusetts.

☐ The only time you can lawfully wear a mask in California is on Halloween.

☐ A fifteenth-century statute under Edward IV of England stated that "no manner of person under the state of a lord shall wear nay gown or mantle, unless it be of such length that he, being upright, it shall cover his buttocks, upon peril to forfeit twenty shillings."

☐ On the South Pacific island of Tonga, no male over six years old is allowed to appear in public without a shirt.

☐ In 1812, a law of Sheffield, England, declared that "under no circumstances whatever shall any preacher be allowed to occupy the pulpit who wears trousers."

☐ A Boston, Massachusetts, law of 1788 prohibited wearing gloves at a funeral.

☐ It is illegal in the African nation of Malawi to wear short pants.

☐ In Hamilton, Ontario, it is illegal to appear on the street after midnight without a full dress suit.

☐ It is against the law to wear white shoes in Tibet.

☐ Moro children of the Philippine Islands are required to wear clothing in school. As soon as school is out, the children tear off their clothes and run off naked.

5

Anyplace
You Hang Your Hat

☐ California law entitles a person to 500 cubic feet of sleeping space in an apartment.

☐ When the Old Newgate jail in Dublin, Ireland, was being torn down and rebuilt on the same spot, a law was enacted stating that the prisoners should remain in the old jail till the new one was completed.

☐ In 1695, a special window tax was imposed in England. All houses that had six or more windows had to pay the tax.

☐ Lodging-house keepers in Boston, Massachusetts, are breaking the law if they put carpeting on the floors or stairways.

☐ In Colonial America, a person was not allowed to live alone.

☐ It is illegal for a married couple in Upton-on-Severn, England, to live in a discarded bus.

☐ In North Carolina, twin beds in a hotel must be separated by at least 2 feet.

SUCH BIG FEET, TOO!

□ Since the eleventh century, females have been forbidden to set foot on Athos, which belongs to a group of monks. This included animals as well as humans, but recently an exception was made, allowing hens and female cats on Athos.

6

Tying the Knot

☐ Claudius II, emperor of Rome in the third century A.D., proclaimed marriage unlawful. He believed that married men made poor soldiers.

☐ A seventeenth-century English law taxed bachelors and widowers over twenty-five years of age a shilling a year while they remained unmarried.

☐ In Baluchistan, a province of Pakistan, a man can legally acquire a wife by exchanging his sister for the woman he wants.

☐ In some ancient Greek states, a penalty was imposed on a man who did not marry and have children.

☐ Until 1871, it was legal in Alabama for a man to choke his wife.

☐ A Pennsylvania law once stated that a husband could not beat his wife after ten o'clock at night.

☐ The Puritans who lived in early New England were not allowed to marry relatives, even those related by marriage. For example, a man could not marry his wife's sister.

☐ In Colonial times, it was against the law for married people not to live together.

☐ In New Hampshire, boys of fourteen and girls of thirteen can legally marry without their parents' consent.

☐ In early Rome, a woman could legally marry at the age of twelve. A man had to wait until he was sixteen.

☐ In Finland, by law, you must know how to read in order to get married.

☐ In some Bantu tribes of West Africa, a marriage is legalized by payment of cattle to the bride's father. If the couple is divorced, the cattle must be returned.

☐ In England's north country, a miner has a common-law right to take his wife to market for sale with a halter around her neck.

☐ In Saudi Arabia, if a man does not keep his wife supplied with coffee, she can divorce him.

☐ A woman in India can legally marry a goat.

☐ In Russia, a couple that is expecting a child or has a child under one year of age cannot get a divorce.

☐ Among some Bantu people, the laws against adultery are so severe that a man can be put to death for merely brushing against the wife of another man as they walk by each other on a path.

7

Generation Gap

☐ Donald Duck comic books were banned from libraries in Finland because authorities felt that it wasn't good to show children a hero who ran around without pants on.

☐ Ann Martin of Newgate, England, was convicted in 1761 of putting out the eyes of children, whom she later took with her to gain sympathy as she begged. Legally, she was punished for damaging the property of others, for the children were not her own. If the children had been hers, she probably would not have been convicted at all.

☐ In Sweden, it is against the law for parents to insult or shame their children.

☐ Until 1814, it was perfectly legal in England to sell your child to beggars.

☐ A child of twelve in Denmark has the legal right to consent to his own adoption.

☐ People of ancient Greece often adopted other adults in order to ensure that they would have heirs.

☐ The government of China permits each married couple to have only one child.

☐ In the United States, parents can legally tell their children what time to go to bed.

8

You Name It

☐ Until recently, French families had to choose names for their children from a list kept by the Ministry of the Interior.

☐ In some parts of the Philippine Islands, it is forbidden to mention the name of anyone living.

☐ If an Athenian father did not wish to keep a baby, he could lawfully leave it on the street to die, as long as it was done before the baby was given a name, at the age of ten days.

☐ In Montana, to claim ownership of a wild animal you have to tattoo your name on it.

☐ In Equatorial Guinea, it is illegal to name any baby Monica.

☐ The Kiowa Indians of North America drop the names of the dead from their language.

☐ When Ireland was ruled by Edward IV of England, the law required every Irishman who resided in the towns of Dublin, Meath, and Kildare to dress like an Englishman, shave his beard above his mouth, and take an English surname.

☐ It is taboo, or forbidden, for Greenland Eskimos to mention their own names.

9

Food for Thought

☐ In Wisconsin, it is against the law to feed margarine, rather than real butter, to prisoners.

☐ According to the laws of the New Haven Colony (Connecticut) in the seventeenth century, it was unlawful to make a mince pie.

☐ The United States Secret Service, known for its diligence in thwarting counterfeiters, once stopped a Philadelphia baker from baking cookies that were designed like U.S. pennies.

☐ Hawaiian women were once put to death for eating coconuts. This food was reserved for men only.

☐ It is illegal in Vermont to add sugar to maple syrup.

☐ In the New Haven Colony (Connecticut), it was against the law to give food or lodging to a Quaker.

☐ Norway prohibits the importing of apples before all its own apples are used up.

☐ In 1548, during the reign of Edward VI, England's Parliament enacted a law forbidding the eating of meat on Friday. This appeared to be for religious reasons but was, in fact, to ensure the sale of fish. It was believed that a boost in the fishing trade would also boost the building of boats, and encourage young men to go to sea—good training for the British navy.

☐ In the Middle Ages, European bakers could be arrested for selling a customer short. To be sure they were not breaking the law, they began adding an extra piece of bread to each order. The "baker's dozen" we hear about today—thirteen pieces in an order for a dozen—grew out of this practice.

☐ It was against the law in the Plymouth Colony (Massachusetts) for a public house of entertainment not to have good beer.

☐ Residents of a Colonial town or village were not permitted to go to the local tavern. Taverns existed for travelers only.

☐ It is against the law in London, England, to hang meat out of your house over the pavement.

☐ Citizens of Locris, in ancient Greece, were breaking the law if they drank wine that was not mixed with water.

10

Shave and a Haircut,
Two Bits

☐ In Michigan, a fourteen-year-old can sue his parents for the right to wear his hair long.

☐ Men in eighteenth-century Spain were not permitted to grow beards, because their king could not grow one.

☐ Alexander the Great, who ruled the Greek empire in the fourth century B.C., ordered his soldiers to shave off their beards. He felt that beards served as convenient handles by which enemies could grab them.

☐ Every male in the New Haven Colony in seventeenth-century America was required by law to "have his hair cut round, according to a cup."

☐ In Elizabethan England, men showing beards of more than two weeks' growth were required to pay a tax.

☐ At one time, Chinese law required all men to wear their hair in long braids as a symbol of submission to their ruler. Those who refused to go along with the humiliating decree (more than a million men) were executed.

11

For Your Own Good

☐ In Kahoka, Missouri, it is unlawful to carry fire through the street unless it is securely covered in a closed vessel.

☐ In Kansas, a physician may prescribe beer for his patient's health, but he cannot join him in drinking it.

☐ It is illegal to deposit dung on a beach in Clacton-on-Sea, England.

☐ In Seattle, Washington, it is illegal to carry concealed weapons over 6 feet in length.

☐ In some English towns, it is an offense to own a bathtub that does not have a watertight plug.

☐ In 1874, a bill was sent to London from Ireland's Parliament for royal approval. It stated that "any member, who from illness or other cause, should be unable to write, might authorize another for him by a writing under his hand."

☐ An old Scottish law, enacted by Parliament in the reign of James I (1424–1437), states that "no man should enter any place where there is hay with a candle."

☐ The president of the United States has a legal right to ride in an armor-plated Pullman railroad car with bullet-proof windows.

☐ The Nebraska legislature made it "unlawful for any person to fire off any pistol . . . on any public road . . . except to destroy some dangerous beast, or an officer in the discharge of his duty."

☐ In the ancient law codes handed down by Hammurabi, king of Babylonia (1792–1750 B.C.), if a doctor failed to cure a patient, his hands were to be cut off.

12

Fair Play

☐ Courts of law in ancient Egypt met in the dark so the judge could not see the defendant, the accuser, or the witnesses, thereby remaining impartial.

☐ During the Middle Ages in Europe, an accused heretic might be subjected to a trial by water, in which his hands and feet were bound and he was thrown into a river. If he sank, this was taken as a sign from God that he was not guilty. If he floated, he was assumed guilty. The trouble was, all those who were proven innocent by this method drowned!

☐ In medieval Europe, it was not uncommon for animals to be tried, convicted, and sentenced for killing human beings. In France, a sow and her six piglets were tried for having killed a child, but only the sow was executed—the judge felt that the piglets were too young to know what they were doing.

□ Butchers were not permitted to serve on juries in medieval Europe. It was assumed that anyone who spent his days killing animals might be insensitive to the taking of any life.

□ In the eighteenth century, women were legally classified with servants, minors, and idiots, and could not be tried for most crimes. The only crimes for which women could be convicted and punished were treason, witchcraft, murder, and being a nagging wife.

□ The Magna Carta, the first book of English law, stated that "No man shall be taken or imprisoned upon the appeal of a woman for the death of any other than her husband."

□ According to the statutes of Edward II of England, "a prisoner who breaks prison is guilty of felony; but if the prison be on fire, this is not so, for he is not to be hanged because he would not stay to be burnt."

13

Dollars and Sense

☐ When Chinese emperor Outi (140–87 B.C.) ran into financial trouble, he had all the white deer in his empire captured and moved to the royal park. Then he passed a law that required anyone entering his court to cover his face with the skin of a white deer, which was available only from the emperor, at considerable cost.

☐ In Omaha, Nebraska, a person receiving an injury due to a defective pavement must advise the city clerk of the facts five days before the accident in order to receive compensation.

☐ United States law allows only a single paper company to manufacture the special paper on which United States currency is printed—Crane & Company of Dalton, Massachusetts. The formula for the paper is kept secret.

☐ Once a United States coin is designed and adopted, it cannot be changed for at least twenty-five years, without special legislation.

☐ A damaged United States bill can be turned in for its full value if three-fifths of it is in good condition.

☐ A lawyer in Clarendon, Texas, must accept eggs, chickens, or other products—as well as money—as payment of legal fees.

☐ People over the age of sixty-five who have received the United States Congressional Medal of Honor for bravery in battle are entitled by law to $10 a month from the federal government.

☐ In the New England colonies, if a debtor had no other means of paying his debts, he could be sold, and the proceeds of the sale used to help pay his bills.

☐ Citizens were, by law, entitled to bring their silver spoons, teapots, and other possessions to the first United States Mint to have them made into coins, free of charge.

☐ In ancient Greece, counterfeiting coins was a crime punishable by death. An official coin tester was appointed to test all coins. Merchants who refused to accept the tested coins had their goods confiscated.

☐ Women of ancient Athens were so extravagant that an official was appointed to prohibit their excessive spending.

☐ A tax collector in ancient Egypt who was found guilty of stealing money from poor people had his nose cut off.

☐ The practice of clipping the edges off coins to make new coins from the shavings was so common in medieval England that all coin-makers were summoned before the king, and those who were unable to prove that they had *not* clipped coins had their right hands cut off.

☐ It was the law in ancient Athens for a rich man to do some public service, such as pay for a ship in the navy, pay the taxes of poor citizens, or pay the expenses of a chorus, which was an important feature of Greek drama.

☐ It was a capital offense in nineteenth-century England to be found passing a forged bank note, even if the bearer had obtained it innocently. The practice so upset famous illustrator George Cruikshank that he created a bank note representing Britannia as a skull, and showing eleven people hanging from scaffolds. The note was "signed" by J. Ketch, the hangman at the time. Copies of the anti-hanging note were widely distributed, leading to increased public outcry about the practice, and soon hanging as a penalty for such a crime was abolished.

14

Let the Punishment
Fit the Crime

☐ According to an early Chinese penal system, the penalty for stealing a horse was to return it to the owner with a bonus of nine additional horses. If the thief could not afford the extra horses, his children might be taken instead. If he had no children, he would be killed.

☐ In Indiana, the law allows a ten-year-old to be executed for committing a capital crime.

☐ The Persian emperor Cyrus the Great once sentenced a river to death because his horse drowned in it.

☐ In ancient Rome, disturbing the peace at night was a crime punishable by death.

☐ An eighteenth-century law of Merrimack, New Hampshire, orders that a person found guilty of adultery be made to stand on a gallows for one hour with a noose around his neck.

☐ In medieval Germany, a man was tried and executed for being a werewolf.

☐ During the Yuan dynasty in China (1271–1368), the most severe penalty—used against those guilty of the most serious crimes such as treason—was death by slow slicing.

☐ In nineteenth-century Great Britain, you could receive the death penalty for committing suicide.

☐ In Athens in the sixth century B.C., you could be put to death for stealing an apple.

☐ In ancient Mexico, the theft of gold or jewels was held to be a crime against Xipe, the Aztec god of spring. Anyone found guilty of this crime became a human sacrifice at the feast honoring Xipe, given by the local goldsmiths.

☐ In thirteenth- and fourteenth-century China, a policeman would be punished with a beating if he had not arrested a thief or a robber for a month.

☐ In sixth- and fifth-century B.C. Athens, one penalty for breaking the law was to be made a slave.

☐ Henry VIII had a special penalty for kitchen help caught in plots to harm their masters: He boiled them in a huge cauldron.

☐ If a counterfeiter escaped from jail in ancient Rome, his jailer could be executed.

☐ An English law during the reign of Elizabeth I stated, "If any person speak any false or slanderous news or tales against the queen, he shall have both his ears cut off."

☐ In some parts of New Zealand, the chief of a tribe is considered sacred. It is strictly taboo to touch him or his belongings. If a person so much as lights a pipe from the chief's fire, he can be put to death.

☐ In sixteenth- and seventeenth-century Europe, a man could be saved from the death penalty if he could read. English poet and playwright Ben Jonson killed an actor in a duel and would have been hanged, but because he could read and write, he merely had an *M* (for murderer) branded on his thumb, a mark he wore all his life.

15

Toil and Trouble

☐ It was unlawful in ancient Greece to be idle.

☐ Under Henry VIII of England, it was legal for old and impotent persons to obtain licenses to beg.

☐ In the early part of the twentieth century, a female schoolteacher in West Virginia was not allowed to marry or date, could not stay out after 8 P.M., and was not permitted to travel outside the city, dress in bright colors, dye her hair, wear fewer than two petticoats, or show more than 2 inches of ankle below her dress.

☐ In North Carolina, it is unlawful to use an elephant to plow a cotton field.

☐ Although private enterprise is now permitted in the Soviet Union, it is forbidden for a private individual or a family to go into the business of manufacturing copying machines.

☐ In Louisiana, you are breaking the law if you are fit and able to work, yet receive support from someone on an old-age pension.

☐ Employees of the first United States Mint in Philadelphia arrived for work early in the morning and were not permitted to leave the building until quitting time—8 P.M.

☐ Each year, men of ancient Egypt were required to prove that they made an honest living; otherwise they could be condemned to death.

☐ New York City horses are entitled by law to a "coffee break." For every two hours of work, they have a fifteen-minute break. And if the temperature goes above 90 degrees Fahrenheit, they get the day off.

☐ Vermont has three legally appointed Fence Viewers, whose job it is to settle boundary disputes between landowners.

☐ In Ohio, it is unlawful to work for an express, telephone, or insurance company whose taxes are more than twenty days overdue.

☐ Among the Ifugao people of Luzon, in the Philippines, it is against the law for outsiders to pass through a rice field while it is being harvested.

☐ It was against the law for a man with legitimate children to become an orator or military officer in ancient Greece.

16

Private Property

☐ In Shawnee, Oklahoma, three or more dogs cannot meet on private property without the consent of the occupant.

☐ Some South Sea island chiefs reserve certain words in their language for themselves, which nobody else is permitted to use.

☐ In the Senchus Mor, the oldest and one of the most important sections of the ancient laws of Ireland, it is written that it is a crime for bees to trespass.

☐ In the Plymouth Colony (Massachusetts), you were breaking the law if you allowed your pigs to wander around without rings in their noses. Pigs without rings could dig up gardens with their snouts.

☐ The law requires that if you build a fence in Vermont, it must be constructed so that sheep cannot escape.

☐ It was a serious crime in ancient Athens for a person to own an olive tree. The trees were considered sacred, and the fruit belonged to the state. The penalty for cutting down an olive tree was death.

☐ Right after World War II, when there was a worldwide gold shortage, it was declared illegal for United States citizens to own gold.

☐ Yugoslavia once forbade Halley's comet from appearing in the heavens over that country.

☐ In Indiana, you must not peep on someone else's property.

☐ It is unlawful for anyone in London, England, to remove sidewalks without permission.

☐ The legislature of Pennsylvania passed a resolution that "The State-House land be enclosed with a brick wall and remain forever an open enclosure."

17

Grave Concerns

☐ In seventeenth-century England, the law required that a dead person be buried in a wool shroud.

☐ In Virginia, you cannot visit a cemetery except to pay respects to the dead.

☐ In the seventh century B.C., a law was passed that no one could be born or die on the Greek island of Delos.

☐ You are breaking the law if you dissect an unclaimed corpse in New York City.

☐ In France, it is legal to lease a grave, instead of buying one. This secures temporary burial for a period of five years. After that, the body may be removed to a factory, where the remaining flesh is boiled off. The resulting skeleton can be sold to a specimen dealer.

☐ According to a Michigan statute of 1883, it is unlawful to have your will probated after you die.

☐ In Boston, Massachusetts, no corpse may be buried except in the hours between sunrise and sunset.

☐ It was unlawful in ancient Rome to injure a dead body in a grave.

☐ A person can purchase a suicide in China for a modest sum. A man suspected of a capital offense may get another man who is innocent to commit suicide, leaving a written confession to the crime committed. The payment takes care of the dead man's family.

☐ You cannot use the color purple in China except for mourning.

☐ In ancient Sparta, where a trim, healthy body and strenuous physical activity were expected of all citizens, the law permitted newborn babies to be examined by elders to see if they met the tough Spartan criteria of physical perfection. Those considered too frail were left to die.

18

Fun and Games

☐ In Purdy, Missouri, dancing—even at a high school prom—is banned in the schools.

☐ In 313, the Roman emperor Constantine declared magic unlawful.

☐ When card games became popular in England, King Henry VIII declared them unlawful. He was afraid that they would draw interest away from archery, his favorite sport.

☐ King Edward III of England banned all sports but archery so that the peasants would become better fighters.

☐ In 1933, a Hollywood movie could not have the word *filthy* in it.

☐ The laws of the New Haven Colony (seventeenth-century Connecticut) prohibited the playing of any musical instrument except for the drum, trumpet, or Jew's harp.

☐ In Massachusetts, "rogues and vagabonds, persons who use any juggling . . . common pipers and fiddlers, may be committed not exceeding six months to the house of correction."

☐ Telling fortunes in Massachusetts is illegal.

☐ It is illegal to copy the makeup used by Universal Studios on the famous monster in the movie *Frankenstein.*

☐ In England, it is unlawful to play any game using dice (with the exception of backgammon), unless you are in a royal palace when a monarch is in residence.

☐ In Scotland, during Mary Stuart's reign, playacting was against the law.

☐ Singing insulting songs was a capital crime in ancient Rome.

☐ It is forbidden to do acrobatics on the sidewalks of Denver, Colorado, that might frighten horses.

☐ In Winchester, Massachusetts, tightrope walking is permitted only in churches.

☐ In 1597, in the time of Queen Elizabeth I, fortune-telling was declared illegal in England. Ever since, fortune-tellers in England have called themselves clairvoyants, whose practice is legal.

☐ In France in 1495, card playing by servants was prohibited by royal decree, except during the Christmas holidays.

☐ Nebraska fishermen must wet their hands when taking fish off their hooks.

☐ In Seattle, Washington, it is illegal to roller-skate in the street.

☐ Dueling is legal in Uruguay—provided both parties are registered blood donors.

☐ In Bhutan, in the Himalayas, fishermen are welcome to catch plenty of fish in its rivers and streams. But since the country is made up of Buddhists, who do not believe in killing any living thing, the fish must be thrown back.

☐ Boxing, considered a brutal Western sport, is outlawed in the People's Republic of China.

☐ You are breaking the law if you play cards for money in Florida.

☐ In eighteenth-century Hawaii, the size of surfboards was regulated by a person's status. The more important the person, the bigger his surfboard. Only a chief could use the largest size, the *olo,* which could be 24 feet long.

19

Never on Sunday

☐ In New York State, it is against the law to practice any public sport, except baseball, on Sunday. It is even unlawful to fish in your own backyard.

☐ In Kansas, you cannot eat rattlesnake meat on Sunday.

☐ In Puritan New England, children were not allowed to play on Sunday. Swings were chained and barred, and only books with religious themes could be read.

☐ In early New England, laws regarding worship and appropriate reverent behavior included these, many of which were later adopted by the other colonies:

parents were not allowed to kiss their children

husbands and wives could not kiss each other

a person could not walk in his garden

one could not make a bed

running was prohibited

cooking was unlawful

it was not permitted to cut one's hair or shave

no one but an authorized clergyman was permitted
    to cross a river

colonists could be put to death for being absent from
    church three Sundays in a row

☐ A law written under England's George III (1738–1820) prohibits "publicly debating on any subject whatsoever on Sunday in any house or place with admission by ticket sold for money."

☐ In 1795, the French passed a law changing the existing French calendar so that each year was divided into twelve months of thirty days each with five extra days at the end of the year. Each month had three ten-day weeks. It created such havoc with feast days and religious observances that it was repealed eleven years later.

☐ Soviet leader Joseph Stalin tried to stamp out the Christmas tree. When his efforts failed, he proclaimed it a New Year's tree.

☐ At one time, women of ancient Athens were not permitted to appear in public except to attend religious festivities.

☐ The religious laws for Muslims are so strict that throughout the month-long holy observance of Ramadan, a Muslim fasts from sunup to sundown, during which time he is not even allowed to swallow his own spit.

20

Law and Order

☐ Residents of Douglas, Wyoming, voted to retain a gallows on their main street.

☐ In Homer, Georgia, only men on the police force can carry slingshots.

☐ In Washington, D.C., no building except the Washington Monument may be higher than the Capitol.

☐ In ancient Persia, anyone found sitting on the king's throne, even by accident, would be put to death.

☐ Until President John F. Kennedy was killed in 1963, it was not a federal felony to assassinate a United States president.

☐ Only one desk is legally reserved in the Senate—the desk that was once used by Daniel Webster. Webster was a native of New Hampshire who represented Massachusetts in the Senate; the resolution reserving the desk was passed on a day when both Massachusetts senators were out of town. The seat went to the senior senator from New Hampshire.

☐ During the reign of Henry VI of England, it was against the law for the sheriff to behead a person who was sentenced to be hanged.

☐ A man could not legally hold a high office in early Rome unless his mother had had a wedding cake broken over her head at her wedding.

☐ During the reign of England's Henry VIII, it was against the law "to practice, or cause to be practiced conjuration, witchcraft, enchantment or sorcery."

21

On the Move

☐ It is unlawful to ride down the street in a motorboat in Brewton, Alabama.

☐ It is against the law to drive past a certain point on Main Street in Newark, Delaware, more than twice in two hours between 8 P.M. and 4 A.M.

☐ In Geneva, New York, it is unlawful to drive up to a gasoline station after dark and tell the attendant to "fill her up."

☐ In California, it is illegal for construction work to block the migration routes of the Santa Cruz long-toed salamander or destroy its habitat.

☐ It is forbidden to take a car into Venice, Italy. You have to park outside the city and walk or take boats to get inside.

☐ It is forbidden in Beijing (Peking), China, to turn your headlights on when driving an automobile at night. It is feared that the lights may blind bicycle riders.

☐ In London, England, it is an unlawful offense for anyone to drive a car without sitting in the front seat.

☐ In London, England, pavements are to be used only for "passing and re-passing."

☐ Kansas law states that "the last car must be left off all trains running within the state of Kansas."

☐ In Wisconsin, it is the law that every railroad passenger car have an ax and a handsaw in plain sight and within reach.

☐ Arizona trains cannot have more than seventy cars, including the caboose.

☐ A New York State law requires that "each train must be preceded by a courier afoot or on a horse," to announce the approaching train.

☐ A book of Irish laws contains one that says "the King's officers may travel by sea from one place to another within the land of Ireland."

☐ Carts were forbidden in the streets of ancient Rome in the daytime, except for those of construction workers.

22

Little Luxuries

☐ Pins were so scarce in twelfth-century England that Parliament passed a law limiting their sale to only two days of the year.

☐ A candidate for office in the United States is legally permitted to say anything he wants to, even if it includes insults and swearwords, when he appears in a political TV commercial.

☐ Mississippi is the only state that does not have a law requiring children to go to school.

☐ For 150 years, starting in 1712, soap was considered a whim of the English aristocracy, and those who used it were required to pay a tax.

☐ According to the laws of Scotland, the right to fish in the deep sea belongs to the public, but salmon fishing belongs only to the Crown.

☐ Under ancient Roman law, a person could wear a gold ring only if he held a military or civil rank. Others could wear silver, but slaves had to wear iron.

☐ In Japan, no one but the imperial family may ride in a maroon car.

Index

Dublin, Ireland, 13
dueling, 54
dung, 28

Edward II, King, 33
Edward III, King, 52
Edward IV, King, 12, 22
Edward VI, King, 24
egg-throwing, 10
Egypt, ancient, 31, 36, 37,
    43
elephant, 10, 43
Elizabeth I, Queen, 40, 53
embracing, 6
England, 3, 4, 11, 13, 17,
    20, 37, 40, 48, 52, 53
Equatorial Guinea, 22
escape (from jail), 40
Europe, 41

fast, 57
fence, 44, 46
Finland, 17, 19
fishing, 24, 54, 55, 64
Florida, 54
food, 23–25, 55
fortune-telling, 52, 53
France, 49, 53
Frankenstein, 52
French, 21, 56
funeral, 12

gallows, 39, 58
games, 52
garbage, 2
gas station, 60
Geneva, New York, 60
George III, King, 56

Germany, 39
gold, 40, 46, 64
gondoliers, 6
grave, 49
Great Britain, 10, 40
Greece, ancient, 17, 20,
    21, 25, 26, 35, 36, 42,
    44, 46
Greenland Eskimos, 22
Greenwich, England, 8

hair, 26–27
Halley's comet, 47
Hamilton, Ontario, 12
Hammurabi, law codes of,
    30
Hawaii, 24, 54
headlights, 61
Henry VI, King, 59
Henry VIII, King, 40, 42,
    51, 59
heretic, 31
hog, 2
Homer, Georgia, 58
horse, 3, 4, 52
hug, 8
human sacrifice, 40
hunters, 10

idleness, 42
impersonating, 4, 8, 9
India, 18
Indiana, 38, 47
insults, 10, 52, 63
Iowa, 5
Ireland, 22, 30, 45, 62

James I, King, 30